The Missing Necklace

Adapted by Lisa Ann Marsoli

Based on the episode "The Amulet of Avalor" by Laurie Israel and Rachel Ruderman

Illustrated by Character Building Studio and the Disney Storybook Art Team

ABDOPUBLISHING.COM

Reinforced library bound edition published in 2019 by Spotlight, a division of ABDO, PO Box 398166, Minneapolis, Minnesota 55439. Spotlight produces high-quality reinforced library bound editions for schools and libraries. Published by agreement with Disney Press, an imprint of Disney Book Group.

Printed in the United States of America, North Mankato, Minnesota.
042018   092018

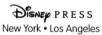

New York • Los Angeles

THIS BOOK CONTAINS
RECYCLED MATERIALS

Library of Congress Control Number: 2017961287

Publisher's Cataloging in Publication Data

Names: Marsoli, Lisa Ann, author. | Israel, Laurie, author. | Ruderman, Rachel, author. | Character Building Studio; Disney Storybook Art Team, illustrators.
Title: Sofia the First: The missing necklace / by Lisa Ann Marsoli, Laurie Israel, and Rachel Ruderman; illustrated by Character Building Studio and Disney Storybook Art Team.
Description: Minneapolis, MN : Spotlight, 2019 | Series: World of reading level 1
Summary: Sofia loses her ability to understand her animal friends when the Amulet of Avalor goes missing and decides to find it. Sofia needs to track down the amulet before Cedric can use it to take over the kingdom.
Identifiers: ISBN 9781532141959 (lib. bdg.)
Subjects: LCSH: Sofia the First (Television program)--Juvenile fiction. | Lost and found possessions--Juvenile fiction. | Amulets--Juvenile fiction. | Human-animal communication--Juvenile fiction. | Readers (Primary)--Juvenile fiction.
Classification: DDC [E]--dc23

Spotlight
A Division of ABDO
abdopublishing.com

There is going to be a ball!
Sofia gets ready.

"I have a surprise!" says King Roland.
"Follow me."

He takes Sofia and Amber to the
Jewel Room.
"Pick out something!" he says.

A baby griffin watches over
the jewels.
Griffins are part lion and part bird.
They love shiny things!

The sisters go to Sofia's room.
The griffin follows.

"Let's try on our jewels," says Amber. Sofia takes off her necklace.

She does not see the griffin.
He flies off with her necklace!

"My necklace!" Sofia cries.
She sees marks on the table.
They are from the griffin's claws.

The girls look for the necklace.

Clover, Mia, and Robin want to help.
Sofia cannot understand them.
She needs her necklace for that!

A maid calls for help.
The gold cups are gone.

The thief left marks behind.

"We will find him!" says the guard.

Cedric sees the griffin outside.
It is wearing Sofia's necklace.

Cedric wants the necklace.
It has special magic.

Cedric tries a spell.
It does not work!

Cedric saves his bird.
The griffin gets away.

Cedric tries again.

He puts a shiny jewel in a trap.

"Now we wait," he says.

The griffin is inside the castle.

Sofia's friends see him.

Too bad they cannot tell Sofia.

The griffin has Sofia's necklace.
Clover grabs it.
The griffin will not let go!

Next the griffin takes Cedric's jewel. The trap does not work.

Cedric grabs for the necklace.
The trap comes down on him!

The queen cannot find her crown.
She sees marks on her table.
She finds a feather, too!

Amber tells her about the other
missing things.

Cedric is still after the griffin.
The griffin loses the jewel.
He loses the crown, too.

Cedric catches them.

Cedric lands in the ballroom.
Everyone sees the jewel and
the crown.

Uh-oh!

They think Cedric took them.

Sofia sees fur and feathers.
She thinks about the claw marks.
Sofia finds the real thief.

The king pets the griffin.

"That tickles!" the griffin says.

Sofia can understand him!

Sofia finds her animal friends.
They have a lot to talk about!